A JIGSAW JONES MYSTERY

The Case of the
Best Pet Ever

A JIGSAW JONES MYSTERY

The Case of the Best Pet Ever

by James Preller

illustrated by Jamie Smith

cover illustration by R. W. Alley

FEIWEL AND FRIENDS

New York

A FEIWEL AND FRIENDS BOOK
An imprint of Macmillan Publishing Group, LLC
175 Fifth Avenue, New York, NY 10010

Our books may be purchased in bulk for promotional, educational, or business
use. Please contact your local bookseller or the Macmillan Corporate and
Premium Sales Department at (800) 221-7945 ext. 5442 or by e-mail at
MacmillanSpecialMarkets@macmillan.com.

Library of Congress Cataloging-in-Publication Data is available.

ISBN 978-1-250-11093-0 (paperback) / ISBN 978-1-250-11092-3 (ebook)

Book design by Véronique Lefèvre Sweet
Illustrations by Jamie Smith

Feiwel and Friends logo designed by Filomena Tuosto

First Feiwel and Friends edition, 2017

Originally published by Scholastic in 2003

Art used with permission from Scholastic

3 5 7 9 10 8 6 4

mackids.com

For Doolin, Seamus, and Daisy—

the dogs in my life

CONTENTS

Chapter 1

Teddy

For the first six days of my life, I didn't have a name. I was the fifth and last kid born in my family. After Billy, Hillary, Nick, and Daniel, my parents couldn't decide on a name for little old me. For six days, I was known as "the baby."

I say this because my mom found a box of old baby pictures today while I was doing a jigsaw puzzle. She got all misty-eyed and blubbery, saying things like, "Goo-goo, ga-ga," and calling me baby names. That is, after she finished yelling at my dog, Rags.

Mom says Rags is a shoe thief. But Ragsy just lies there, sprawled on the carpet. He can't figure out what the fuss is about. I think it's kind of funny. But Mom is missing three different shoes and she doesn't think it's funny at all.

So anyway, for six days my parents called me "the baby." They figured the right name would pop into their heads. By day four, the names that had popped into my dad's head were Carlos, Lars, Ferdinand, and Slippy.

(I think he was.)

Mom said, "No, No, NO!" and "Slippy?! Are you *trying* to make me crazy?!"

On day six, she said that I was as cute as a teddy bear.

"Sure," my dad agreed. "A bald, pink, wrinkled teddy bear."

So they named me Teddy, even though my official name is Theodore Andrew Jones.

No one ever called me Teddy, though. And that's a good thing—since Teddy isn't a great name for a detective. A boy detective should be named Nick or Sam or Derek or Roscoe. You know, a cool, tough-sounding name.

Anyway, now I'm in second grade. And these days everybody calls me Jigsaw, except for my brothers, who usually call me Worm and Shorty.

I got the nickname because I love jigsaw puzzles. But the one thing I like more than doing jigsaw puzzles is solving mysteries. See, I'm a detective. And I've got the decoder ring to prove it.

I have a partner, too. Her name is Mila (sounds like "my-la"). We've found missing hamsters, stolen bicycles, and disappearing dinosaurs. We've had cases with spooky ghosts, marshmallow monsters, and walking scarecrows.

It's how we earn our living.

"For a dollar a day, we make problems go away."

It beats selling Kool-Aid for a living.

"You really did look like a teddy bear," Mom gushed. She held up my baby photo. "Don't you agree?"

Woof-woof, woof!

Thanks to Rags, I didn't have to answer. Rags is like a walking doorbell with fur and a wet tongue.

I figured Mila was at the door. There was a big case brewing and we needed to talk. Bobby Solofsky had called that afternoon. He said he wanted to hire us and he was coming over to explain.

It would take a lot of explaining.

Bobby Solofsky has been a stone in my shoe since kindergarten. He's always bragging about how he's a better detective than I am. So why, I wondered, would he want to hire us?

There was definitely something fishy here—and it wasn't my tuna sandwich.

Chapter 2

Grand Prize Gone!

I can always tell when Mila's coming. Her singing enters the room two minutes before she does. Today she was singing "Where, Oh, Where Has My Little Dog Gone," only she changed the words around.

"Why, oh, why did Solofsky call?
What, oh, what could he want?"

I was glad to see her. This Solofsky thing was bugging me. We needed to talk before he showed up.

Before Mila could say anything, I put my finger to my nose. That was our secret signal. Billy (my favorite brother) was sprawled on a living room chair, talking to his new girlfriend. Get this—her name is Rain. Not Snow, not Sleet, but Rain. She sounded like a drip to me.

We went to my tree house for privacy.

"Spill it," Mila said. "Why does Solofsky want to hire us?"

"No idea," I answered. "But I do know this. Bobby Solofsky can't be trusted. I don't want anything to do with this case."

Mila frowned, pulling on her long black hair. "This is business," she said. "It's not personal. We should hear what he's got to say."

I guessed she was right.

Suddenly, Rags started barking. Solofsky was here. I downed a glass of grape juice and wiped my mouth.

Bobby Solofsky climbed the tree house ladder. His face was a scowl. I waited for him to speak. But he just sat there. The minutes crawled by like lazy cockroaches.

"So?" I said.

"So?" he replied.

Mila started to hum. She couldn't help herself. "A needle pulling thread," she sang.

I ignored her.

"Time is money, Solofsky," I said. "What's up?"

He grunted and shrugged. Then he ran his tongue across the front of his teeth and made a gross sucking sound. I've known camels with better manners.

"First off," Solofsky began, "I'd solve this case myself, but I'm not allowed at the scene of the crime."

I scratched the back of my neck and listened.

"Start from the beginning," Mila urged. "Tell us everything you remember."

I opened my detective journal.

"I have to clear my good name," Solofsky said angrily. "That guy in the store blamed me for no reason. I put the medal back exactly where I found it!"

"Slow down," I told Solofsky. "What guy? What store? What medal?"

I poured him a glass of grape juice. That seemed to calm him down. "Here's the deal," Solofsky said. "One, I was in that new pet store last Saturday. Two, the grand prize for their animal talent show was on the counter. I picked it up. Then I put it right back down. Now the owner says I stole it."

"What did he say, exactly?" I prodded.

Solofsky groaned. "He said, 'You should return the medal before your aura turns black.'"

"Your aura?" I repeated.

"The guy is a little weird," Bobby answered. He wagged a finger in a circular motion beside his ear. "He's bonkers. He's a Froot Loop, I tell ya. And I've been framed!"

I frowned at Bobby's description. His words left a bad taste in my mouth.

"Tell us more about this pet shop," Mila said.

"It's crazy," Solofsky scoffed. "There's this really loud-talking parrot. And animals run around free. Like, um, there's a cat and a ferret."

I glanced down at my notes. "Let me get this straight, Solofsky. You're not allowed in the store because the owner thinks you stole some kind of medal. Is that right?"

Solofsky nodded.

"And you want to hire us to help clear your name?"

"That's right," Solofsky said.

"When is the contest?" Mila asked. "And is this medal the grand prize?"

"I was getting to that," Solofsky snorted. "It's an animal talent show. The contest is this Saturday. The winner gets this cool gold medal. I figure it's worth a few bucks, for sure," he added.

I looked Solofsky in the eye. "I've got to ask," I said. "Did you take it?"

"No way," he blurted.

"One more thing," I said. "Why do you care if you're not allowed in the store? You don't even have a pet."

Bobby tapped his foot. His eyes narrowed. "There is this little white puppy," he confessed. "She's kind of cute and I like to visit her. You know, play with her and stuff."

I'll admit it. That surprised me. I never figured Solofsky for the cute puppy type.

A scream came from my house. It was my mom again. "Rags!" she hollered.

Another shoe was missing.

I locked eyes with Mila. Then I pushed a glass jar toward Solofsky. "We'll look into it for you," I promised. "Three dollars ought to be enough to get us started."

"Three dollars?!" Solofsky protested.

I shrugged. "That's the price, pal. Hire us, or don't hire us. It makes no difference to me."

Solofsky grumbled, muttered, and moaned. Then he shoved three crumpled dollars in the jar.

Chapter 3

Fur, Fins & Feathers

It was time to take a little trip to the pet store. My brother Billy was happy to drive Mila and me. We brought Rags along for the ride. Billy never missed a chance to borrow my mom's car. Besides, he told me, his girlfriend worked there.

"Rain?" I asked.

He nodded.

"What kind of name is that?" Mila asked.

"Her parents are a little . . . different," Billy explained.

"No kidding," I answered. "Does she have a sister named Partly Cloudy?"

"Har-har, detective," Billy groaned. He pulled up the car in front of the store.

"Come on, Rags," I said. "We've got a little detective work to do."

It was good for Rags to get out of the house. He'd been making my mom a little crazy lately. I figured the pet store owner might give me some advice on how to solve Ragsy's shoe problem. It was the perfect cover. No one would suspect Mila and I were really snooping around for clues.

There was a sign over the door.

> FUR, FINS & FEATHERS

I pulled off my baseball cap and scratched my head. "Kind of a weird name," I murmured to Mila as we stepped inside.

"Hi, Billy!" A tall girl with white teeth and twinkling eyes waved to my brother from behind the counter.

"Who-o-o-oa!" a shaggy-haired man exclaimed. "My daughter and I were just talking about you, Billy, and like, wow, here you are!" He snapped his fingers in astonishment. As if Billy walking in the door was the most amazing thing that had ever happened.

Go figure.

"Hey, Jax," Billy said, squeezing my shoulder. "This is my little brother Jigsaw. He's looking for some advice."

"Far out," Jax said. "Billy's little bro."

Okay, confession time: I wasn't exactly honest with Billy about the case. After all, his girlfriend was a suspect. That's the thing in my line of work. Everybody's a suspect, and anything is possible. It can put a detective in a tight spot. I didn't want Billy to know that I was checking out a robbery—and that his own girlfriend might be the thief. After all, she was at the scene of the crime.

"Where are my glasses?" Jax patted his pockets, scratched his head, and looked

around the store. "The animal kingdom is full of sticky-fingered critters. I love it! Where's my green tea?" He wandered off, searching for his lost cup of tea.

Mila and I made eye contact. Neither of us had a clue about what Jax had just said. Mila nodded at a sign above the counter.

"Wow," I said, pointing to the sign. "You're having a talent show?"

Rain drew her lips together in a tight frown. "Yes, but," she said, "the grand prize is missing. My father thinks a boy took it this weekend."

"Were there witnesses?" I asked.

"Not exactly," Rain said. "I saw the boy holding the prize. And the next minute, it was gone."

"What will you do without a prize?" Mila asked. She poked me with her elbow and crept off to look around the store.

"We'll think of something," Rain said.

I tried to keep Rain talking while Mila checked out the store.

"Maybe I can solve the mystery for you." I pulled out my detective journal. "Give me the facts," I said.

Rain smiled at me. "Well, okay. Why not? There was an older couple looking at the fish. And there was a girl named Danika who was upset about the animals in cages. . . ."

"Animals in cages! Animals in cages!" a high-pitched voice squawked. I turned and saw a parrot pacing on a stand, screaming its head off. *"Cages! Cages!"* it repeated over and over.

Suddenly, a cat and a ferret raced over my shoes, through my legs, and across the floor.

Rags leaped up and strained at his leash.

"Sorry." Rain laughed. "The cat's name is Rainbow, and this is Curiosity, our ferret. They're both free to roam around the store." Rain picked up the ferret and gently stroked its head. The ferret reached up and playfully batted at Rain's earring.

Meanwhile, Rags was pretty much flipping out. He whined and pulled on his leash. "*Shhh*, Rags," I said. "It's okay."

Mila pointed to a photograph on the wall of Rain and her family. She called me over. "Look at this, Jigsaw," Mila said with a laugh. "The ferret is sitting on that lady's head!"

Solofsky was right about one thing. This sure was a lively little store. "That Jax," I whispered. "He's a little . . ."

"Colorful?" Mila suggested.

"Yeah," I agreed. "And nobody actually saw Bobby take the prize. As strange as this might seem, Solofsky might be telling the truth."

Woof, woof! Rags pawed at me in alarm. The ferret, Curiosity, was trying to tackle his tail.

Jax quickly came over. "It's cool, Jigsaw, no worries," he cooed calmly. "Ferrets are active little critters. They're always into something. But they sure make life interesting!"

It was time to go. Between the squawking and the meowing and the barking, I'd had enough of the wonders of nature for one day. I needed peace and quiet so I could think. At Jax's suggestion, I bought a cheap chew toy for Rags. Maybe this would keep him from stealing Mom's shoes.

Behave!

Guess who wasn't talking about the animal talent show at school the next day?

Nobody!

And I was getting worried. If I didn't find the missing prize, Solofsky would tell everyone that I couldn't crack the case. I wondered if Solofsky was setting me up. This could all be another one of his tricks to make me look bad.

Before the morning bell, kids were lying on the reading rug, talking at desks, or just hanging around. By the cubbies, I heard

Lucy Hiller tell Mila that she was planning to enter the contest. "But before I finished filling out the form in the store, I noticed my glitter purse was missing." Lucy complained, "I still don't know what happened to it."

Hmmm. That made for two robberies at Fur, Fins & Feathers. I wondered if the person who took the grand prize also stole Lucy's purse.

Joey Pignattano walked in the door. He looked like he'd just lost a fight with a wolverine. He had scratches all over his hands and face.

"What happened to you?" I asked.

"Four words, Jigsaw," Joey said, glumly holding up four fingers. "Never dress a cat."

"Eyes are—" Ms. Gleason stood at her desk and waited for us to answer her.

"WATCHING!" some of us answered.

"Ears are—"

"LISTENING!" more of us answered.

he does have some interesting behaviors. Which brings us to our next assignment. I want each of you to choose an animal and list four interesting ways in which that animal behaves. Use your own pet if you have one."

Oh, great, I thought. Rags in action. He sleeps. He drools. He sleeps some more. I scribbled a quick picture, including a puddle of slime.

"I saw some really cool snakes at the zoo on Saturday," Eddie Becker blurted out. "Can I use them?"

"Yes, you may choose any animal you like," Ms. Gleason answered. "Even our class hamster!"

Just before recess, I got a secret message from Mila.

MT M T TH TR SWNG. HV NWS.

"So, what's up?" I asked Mila on the playground. I held up her coded message and read, "Meet me at the tire swing. I have news." It was one of our favorite codes. Mila had left out all the vowels!

"Rain was right," Mila said. "Danika was in the pet store at the time of the robbery. She was protesting the treatment of the animals."

"Huh?"

"Danika thinks some of the cages are too small," Mila explained.

My list of suspects was growing. Danika Starling is room 201's biggest animal lover. I wondered if she was mad enough at the pet store to steal.

"I've got an idea," Mila said. "You should enter Rags in the contest."

"Rags? In a *talent* show?" I laughed. "Rags is a good dog, but he doesn't exactly have any talents."

"It will get you behind the scenes," Mila urged. "It might help us break the case."

"Yeah," I muttered. "And I'll get laughed at when Rags sleeps through the whole thing!"

Chapter 5

The Case of the Missing Talent

"Little Holmes!" Jax greeted me when I walked in the store.

"Hi, Jigsaw," Rain said. "I was just telling Dad that you're a detective. Are you here to solve the mystery?"

"Actually, my mom is parked outside," I said. "I just want to enter Rags in the contest."

"Awesome, Little Holmes!" Jax shouted again.

"Dad loves Sherlock Holmes," Rain explained.

I nodded politely and tried to put a smile on my face. Little Holmes? *Yuck.* Theodore was bad enough. I didn't need another name. "You can call me Jigsaw," I suggested.

Jax was a suspect. By pretending that the grand prize was stolen, he wouldn't have to spend money on a giveaway. It was definitely a motive. The oldest one in the world, in fact. Money.

I went over the list of suspects. Rain said the older couple never even came to the front counter. So they couldn't have done it.

That left four suspects: Solofsky, Danika, Jax, and Rain. I needed proof. Hard facts. Right now, it was like trying to do a puzzle with some of the pieces missing.

"What talent does your dog have?" Rain asked.

"That's the problem," I grumbled. "He doesn't seem to have one."

Rain pinched her lower lip thoughtfully.

"All animals have talent. You could give Rags a doggy IQ test," she suggested.

"Brilliant idea!" Jax cheered. He fished around the cluttered counter until he found a magazine article. He handed it to me. The headline read: HOW SMART IS YOUR DOG?

"Thanks," I said, shoving the magazine into my backpack.

Squawk! "Funny ferret! Funny ferret!"

I nearly jumped out of my socks in surprise. "Yowza!" I exclaimed.

Rainbow and Curiosity, the cat and the ferret, darted across the floor. *Clang, ka-boom!* They knocked over a display of cat toys.

Rain looked at me and laughed. "It's just the animals."

Squawk. "Just the animals! Just the animals!" echoed the parrot.

Rain excused herself to see to another customer. That's when I got a crazy idea. I walked up to Polly the parrot. "Okay, my

feathered friend," I whispered to Polly. "It looks like you're my only witness. Tell me. Do you think Rain took the prize?"

Squawk. *"Rain took the prize! Rain took the prize!"*

"Good work, Little Holmes!" Jax shouted happily. "You've solved the mystery! Far-out!"

"Very funny, Dad," Rain said. "Polly only repeats what she hears!"

I laughed it off, too. Very funny. Ha-ha. But deep down inside, I had a feeling that Polly was trying to tell me something.

"Hey, Dad, have you seen my sparkly hair clip?" Rain asked Jax. "I'm sure I left it here on the counter."

I suddenly noticed Bobby Solofsky staring inside the store, his nose smushed against the front window. He looked sad and lonely. After I filled in the contest entry form, I went outside to talk to him.

"How's Bubbles?" he asked me.

"Bubbles?"

"The white puppy," he said. "Does she seem happy?"

"Sure, Solofsky," I said. "I guess so. I mean, about as happy as a puppy in a pet store can be. But between us, I think Bubbles needs a boy."

Solofsky's face brightened. "You do?"

"Every puppy needs a kid," I said. "Don't you know that?"

I headed toward my mom's car. Rain's sparkly hair clip was missing. And Bobby Solofsky hadn't even been in the store. Neither was Danika.

Very interesting.

Chapter
6

IQ Test

Rain and Billy showed up at my house like two little lovebirds, arm in arm.

Yuck.

"You're just in time for the doggy IQ test," I told them.

Mila read aloud from the magazine. "It says here that the best way to measure your dog's IQ is to test his problem-solving skills. It also says that smart dogs obey well."

"Sit!" I commanded Rags. He wagged his tail and barked.

"Well, he's awake," Billy noted cheerfully. Rain giggled.

"Hey, Rain," I asked. "I was wondering. Do you know what the missing grand prize was worth?"

Billy eyed me closely.

"I sure do," Rain answered. "Dad told me it cost forty-five dollars."

Sometimes a detective has to stir things up just to see how they fall. Half smiling, I asked Rain: "You didn't take the grand prize for yourself, did you?"

Billy gave me a funny look. "Hey, what are you asking, Jigsaw?"

Rain smiled. "It's okay, Billy. Jigsaw is a detective. He has to look at all the possible suspects."

I could see why Billy liked her.

"Believe me, Jigsaw," Rain said. "I'm not happy about this missing prize, either. After all, the talent show was my idea."

"It could be more than one person," I said. "Anything is possible."

Solofsky sighed. He gathered up the comic books and carelessly threw them on his bedside table. They toppled over onto the carpet.

He suddenly turned and looked at us with desperate eyes. "You've gotta help me," he pleaded. "I've got to be allowed back in that store. Jigsaw, Mila—you're my last hope."

Chapter 8

Tricky Business

Before class started on Friday morning, I sat down at my desk to read through my detective journal. But it was hard to think. Everyone was talking about the talent show.

Kim Lewis was training a jumping frog. Nicole Rodriguez claimed she had a cat that could do backflips. Helen Zuckerman wouldn't stop talking about her poodle. She said it spoke French.

Joey had, thankfully, given up the idea of dressing his cat. Instead, he was trying to train a worm to roll over.

"How's it coming along?" I asked Joey.

He shrugged. "It's hard. Wormy doesn't understand me. I don't think he has ears."

I closed my notebook and got out my animal behavior folder. I'd been so busy with the case that I hadn't done the homework. I started a list:

RAGS
1. He sleeps.
2. He drools.
3. He barks at the doorbell.

I tapped my eraser and tried to think of a good number four. I thought about what we do when Rags and I are together. The truth is, Rags doesn't do much. But somehow, he's good company anyway. I started to write "good company," but I erased it. It wasn't really a behavior.

Then I thought about our training sessions. Rags had learned to pick up a shoe

on command, but he always missed the box
when he set it down. I added to my list:

> 4. He never gets things where
>   he means to put them.

That was it! I suddenly realized Bobby
and Rags had something in common.

I scribbled a coded message and passed
it to Mila:

W MST G T TH STR FTR SCHL.
THNK KNW WHR TH PRZ S!

She read it, smiled, and rubbed a finger
across her nose. "We must go to the store
after school. I think I know where the prize
is!" She got the message!

Chapter 9

The Hiding Place

I had the answer and it didn't get anyone in trouble! The thief wasn't Rain or Jax or Bobby. At least, not really Bobby. Not on purpose, anyway.

"Hi, Jax!" I called out as Mila and I walked into the store on Friday afternoon.

"Mila! Little Holmes! What's up?" Jax greeted us.

"Jigsaw thinks he may have solved the case," Mila said proudly.

"Far-out!" Jax exclaimed.

I got down on my hands and knees and searched the floor. I was sure Bobby had meant to put the prize back on the counter, but missed. I'd seen him do the same thing when putting stuff away in his room. He was careless with the Legos, and they fell. Same thing with the comic books. Bobby is just like Rags! *They never get things where they mean to put them!*

I was sure that the prize had fallen to the floor and got kicked under the counter.

But I was wrong. There was nothing there but some dust bunnies. It hadn't even been swept out lately.

"Rats!" I muttered.

"Last cage on the left," Jax said.

"No," I said. "I mean *rats*! I was wrong. Rats!"

"Rats! Rats!" the parrot squawked.

A woman at the counter looked startled.

"It's cool, ma'am," Jax reassured her. "No rats on the loose. Just a talking parrot!"

Suddenly, Rainbow and Curiosity made one of their mad dashes through the store. Curiosity stopped, spun, and began to nibble on the silver buckle of the woman's shoe.

Naturally, the woman screamed.

The parrot kept squawking, *"Rats! Rats!"*

The woman, looking flustered, patted her pockets. "My keys," she said, looking around the store in alarm. "I don't seem to have my keys!"

One more mystery to solve!

That night, I was as frustrated as a dentist in a candy store. I still had no answers for the case. There was a robber in that pet store, all right. But I couldn't figure out who it was.

I decided to work on the trick with Rags. I gave him a shoe and pointed to the box.

"Rags!" I yelled. "Don't just drop it on the floor!"

My dad stuck his head in from the kitchen. "Having a tough time with old Rags?"

"He's hopeless!" I complained. "What a useless dog!"

Right away, I felt bad for saying it.

Even Rags seemed to understand. He looked at me with hurt eyes.

"I guess you haven't been able to teach that old dog a new trick," my father said. He gave Rags a friendly pat.

"No, I haven't," I growled.

"Well, don't give up on Rags. He'll learn.

It just may take some time. Besides, Rags thinks you're about the greatest person on the planet. Look how he watches you, Jigsaw," Dad said.

I looked at Rags. And he looked at me. And I remembered all the good times we had together. Squirting him with a hose. Pretending he was a turkey and chasing him around the yard on Thanksgiving. Sleeping together in my bed, snug and warm.

That's what he did best of all, I realized. The big fur ball loved me with all his heart. Every minute of every hour of every day.

And that's no small trick.

My father patted me on the shoulder. "A wise man once said, 'Try to be the person your dog thinks you are.'"

He smiled and headed back into the kitchen. "I have an important meeting with a cheesecake," he explained. Rags followed him. Rags liked cheesecake, too.

Later that night, after I finished my spelling homework, I grabbed a plastic bag. It was time to walk Rags. But I could only find one of my sneakers.

"Rags," I muttered to myself. "Now he's going after *my* shoes."

I wanted to catch him in the act. I looked high. I looked low. No Rags. I tried the basement. Nothing. When I started back upstairs I heard a noise. I pushed open the door to the furnace room.

That's where I saw his tail poking out from behind the furnace.

"Hey, boy," I called sweetly.

Rags popped his head out. My Nike was in his mouth, covered with drool.

"Gross!" I said. I climbed behind the furnace to grab the shoe.

That's when I saw it. His stash. Four of Mom's missing shoes—and about seventeen socks that I didn't even know were missing.

They were all shoved in a dark corner behind the furnace.

Ragsy's treasure.

Chapter 10

Suspects by the Dozen!

I realized that my dog's hiding place was the missing piece of the puzzle. Faster than a dog can steal a shoe, it was clear that I had missed dozens of possible suspects. They were all at the scene of the crime—and they were still there!

It was Saturday. The day of the contest. Mila met me at the store. When Rags and I got there, it was already crowded. Animals were barking and screeching and hissing. Rain was putting the finishing touches on the stage in front of the counter. Folding chairs were set up all the way to the door. The place was a zoo!

"What's up?" Mila said when she saw me.

Woof! Woof!

I held tight to Ragsy's leash.

"Rags gave me a clue!" I said. I told her what I had discovered. "He can't be the only animal in the world that likes to hide things."

"But which animal is it?" Mila asked. "There must be dozens of suspects in the store."

Then she snapped her fingers. Mila ran to the photograph on the wall. "Remember Rain's hair clip?" she exclaimed. "I bet that ferret was going after the clip in this woman's hair!"

Sure enough, Mila was right. In the photo with the ferret atop the woman's head, we could see part of a clip in the ferret's paws.

"Jax did say ferrets were always getting into trouble," I remembered. "But we weren't paying attention."

"Now for the hard part," Mila said. "We have to find the ferret's hiding place!"

Rags and I headed to the back of the store. Mila took the front. Rags was panting and pulling on his leash. More kids were

showing up. The show was minutes away
and the ferret was nowhere to be seen.

Mila shook her head as we met at the
stage. "I asked Jax to help us," she said. "But
Curiosity isn't in any of his usual places."

The seats were filling up. Ms. Gleason waved
at me. Danika was talking to Jax. It seemed
like everyone from room 201 was in the store.

"Any luck?" Rain asked me hopefully.

I frowned.

"That's okay," she said with a smile. "At least you tried. And the show must go on. You and Rags are last. Right after Wingnut O'Brien's hamster act."

My stomach flipped and my knees flopped. Rags and I were about to go down in history as the worst pet trick ever. Mila found a seat. She held on to Rags while I searched the supply closet.

"Welcome to the First Annual Fur, Fins & Feathers Talent Show!" Rain announced. Everybody cheered. I stood in the dark closet and tried to think like a ferret.

It wasn't easy.

I looked behind the bags of dog food. In the distance, I heard Helen's poodle bark in French—*Oui! Oui! Oui!*

Lucy Hiller went, then Joey with his crazy worm trick. One by one, I heard contestants show off their pets as the crowd cheered. I looked behind every bag, box, and can. No ferret.

"Wingnut O'Brien and his hamster, Hermie!" I heard Rain announce.

Rags and I were next. He had never once done his trick and the grand prize was still missing. I felt like a failure.

I headed back to Mila and Rags. Wingnut was singing a duet with Hermie. The hamster squeaked along to "Mary Had a Little Lamb." The crowd roared with laughter.

Just great, I thought. Rags and I have to follow the best act in the show.

Chapter
11

Rags to Riches

Squawk! Squawk! Squawk!

Polly the parrot was screeching at the top of her lungs. The cat and ferret tore through the crowd, climbing up on seats, diving, leaping, scrambling over everything in sight.

My heart leaped. Curiosity had something in its mouth.

"Hey!" Ms. Gleason cried. "That ferret stole my earring!"

Mila raced up to me. "The parrot is like an alarm system," she exclaimed. "When the ferret steals something, the parrot squawks!"

We took off after the ferret with Rags leading the way. We followed them down the dog toys aisle and around a corner. But Rags barked and Mila and I stopped short. Curiosity had vanished.

Rain tried to calm down the crowd.

"Out of control, Little Holmes!" Jax laughed. "Where'd the little critter go?"

"Thin air," I muttered.

That's when Rags did the most amazing thing. He sniffed the floor, stood on his hind legs, and barked at some dog beds on a shelf.

Loudly.

Over and over again.

"Crazy dog!" Jax said gleefully. He reached his arm up and the ferret jumped onto his shoulder. Jax smiled and pulled down a big stuffed dog bed.

There on the bed lay a bunch of shiny objects, including Rain's hair clip, a set of keys, a shiny purse, an earring, and the grand-prize medal!

Jax held up the prize. "Rock on, Little Holmes! You solved the mystery!"

Rain clapped her hands together. Ms. Gleason gave me a thumbs-up. And Rags rested his bones on the cool tile floor.

I glanced toward the front window. Sure enough, there was Solofsky, nose pressed against the glass.

Jax saw Solofsky, too. "Excuse me," Jax said. "I have an apology to make."

Rain gave me a big hug. "You're a hero, Jigsaw!"

Nope, I thought. Rags was the real hero. It seemed wrong to ask him to do a silly shoe trick after such great detective work. But people were pushing us toward the stage and cheering.

Rain set out a box and an old shoe. Mila gave me a push toward the stage. Rags and I were about to go from hero to zero!

I looked Rags in the eye. He looked back at me like he thought I was the best person on the planet. I wasn't, but I didn't argue with Rags. I heard my father's voice in my head. *Try to be the person your dog thinks you are.* So I took a deep breath, looked at Rags with all the love in my heart, and said, "Steal the shoe, Ragsy."

Rags picked up the shoe in his mouth. He walked across the stage. He looked at me once, then dropped the shoe into the box.

As if he'd done it a thousand times.
The crowd exploded.

I couldn't believe it.

My old dog had learned a new trick!

In the end, Wingnut and his hamster won the contest. That was okay. Everybody knew Rags was the best pet ever.

"I should have figured it out," Rain said. "Ferrets are known for their sneaky behavior. Hiding things is not a surprise."

I saw Jax talking with Bobby. Jax was leaning close to him, speaking softly, shaking his hand. Bobby had a huge grin on his face. He raced over to Bubbles and they tumbled on the floor together.

"Guess you're off the hook," I said to Bobby.

"Not only that," Bobby bragged. "I just got a job as a dog walker."

I waited for him to thank me. But he didn't. Solofsky just played with his puppy. Happy as can be.

"You're welcome," I finally said.

"Oh, right," Bobby replied. "Thanks, Jigsaw. Too bad it took you so long, but I guess you tried pretty hard."

Yeesh.

Zebras never change their stripes. And Solofsky will always be a stone in my shoe.

But none of it mattered. The case was solved. Rags thought I was the best person in the world. And I felt the same way about him.

solve. That's because I know the secret. The simple trick? Don't give up.

Don't ever give up.

My dog, Rags, leaped at the door. He barked and barked. A minute later, the doorbell rang. *Ding-a-ling, ding-dong.* That's the thing about Rags. He's faster than a doorbell. People have been coming to our house all his life. But for my dog, it's always the most exciting thing that ever happened.

Every single time.

"Get the door, Worm," my brother Billy said. He was sprawled on the couch, reading a book. Teenagers, yeesh.

"Why me?" I complained.

"Because I'm not doing it."

Billy kept reading.

Rags kept barking.

And the doorbell kept ringing.

Somebody was in a hurry.

I opened the door. Joey Pignattano and

Danika Starling were standing on my stoop. We were in the same class together, room 201, with Ms. Gleason.

"Hey, Jigsaw!" Danika waved. She bounced on her toes. The bright beads in her hair clicked and clacked.

"Boy, am I glad to see you!" Joey exclaimed. He burst into the room. "Got any water?"

"I would invite you inside, Joey," I said, "but you beat me to it."

Danika smiled.

"I ate half a bag of Jolly Ranchers this morning," Joey announced. "Now my tongue feels super weird!"

"That's not good for your teeth," I said.

Joey looked worried. "My tongue isn't good for my teeth? Are you sure? They both live inside my mouth."

"Never mind," I said.

"Pipe down, guys!" Billy complained. "I'm reading here."

"Come into the kitchen," I told Joey and Danika. "We'll get fewer complaints. Besides, I've got grape juice. It's on the house."

"On the house?" Joey asked. "Is it safe?"

I blinked. "What?"

"You keep grape juice on your roof?" Joey asked.

Danika gave Joey a friendly shove. "Jigsaw said 'on the house.' He means it's free, Joey," she said, laughing.

Joey pushed back his glasses with an index finger. "Free? In that case, I'll take a big glass."

Chapter 2

One Small Problem

I poured three glasses of grape juice.

"Got any snacks?" Joey asked. "Cookies? Chips? Corn dogs? Crackers?"

"Corn dogs?" I repeated. "Seriously?"

"Oh, they are delicious," Joey said. "I ate six yesterday. Or was that last week? I forget."

Danika shook her head and giggled. Joey always made her laugh.

I set out a bowl of chips.

Joey pounced like a football player on a

fumble. He was a skinny guy, but he ate like a rhinoceros.

"So what's up?" I asked.

"We found a note," Danika began.

"Aliens are coming," Joey interrupted. He chomped on a fistful of potato chips.

I waited for Joey to stop chewing. It took a while. *Hum-dee-dum, dee-dum-dum.* I finally asked, "What do you mean, aliens?"

"Aliens, Jigsaw!" he exclaimed. "Little green men from Mars—from the stars—from outer space!"

I looked at Danika. She shrugged, palms up. "Maybe," she said. "You never know."

I took a long swig of grape juice. "You mentioned a note," I said to Danika.

She sat tall, eyes wide. "It's very mysterious, Jigsaw. That's why we came to you."

"Narffle-snarffle," Joey mumbled, his mouth still full of chips.

I leaned back in my chair. I shoved my hands into my pockets. They were empty. Business had been slow. I was a detective without a case. "Let me make a phone call," I said.

I never work alone. My partner's name is Mila Yeh. We split the money down the middle, fifty-fifty. Mila has long black hair. She's crazy about books. And she's my best friend on the planet. Together, we make a good team.

I asked Mila to meet us in my tree house. She said she'd be over in five minutes.

It took her three and a half.

Mila lived next door. And she was as quick as a rabbit.

As usual, Mila was singing. I knew the tune, but the words were different:

"Twinkle, twinkle, little mystery!
How I wonder what you are!
Could you really be up there?
Do Martians wear . . . underwear?"

"You're funny," Danika said. She beamed a warm smile in Mila's direction.

Grinning, Mila sat down, crisscross applesauce. We gathered in a snug circle. There was no choice. My tree house wasn't exactly a palace. I am not complaining. But I don't go up there on windy days. Mila's eyes were active and alert. They moved from Joey to Danika, before settling on me. "Aliens, huh?" Mila asked.

"From outer space," Joey said.

"Uh-huh," Mila replied. If she thought Joey was crazy, Mila was too nice to say it out loud.

I took out my detective notebook. I opened to a clean page. With a blue pen, I wrote:

THE CASE FROM OUTER SPACE
CLIENTS: Joey and Danika
CLUES:

I left the last part blank. I didn't have any clues. I wasn't even sure I had a case. But it was better than nothing.

"Maybe we could start from the beginning," Mila suggested.

"Hold on." I slid forward an empty coin jar. "We get a dollar a day."

Joey and Danika exchanged glances. "We have one teensy-weensy problem," Danika said.

Uh-oh.